1987

THE YEAR
I WAS BORN

A Daily Record of Events
Canadian Edition

Compiled by LINDA GRANFIELD
Illustrated by BILL SLAVIN

BIRTH CERTIFICATE

Name: _____

Birthdate: _____

Time: _____

Place: _____

Weight: _____

Length: _____

Mother's name: _____

Father's name: _____

Kids Can Press Ltd.
Toronto

for Val Wyatt,
always a patient and generous guide
through the non-fiction jungle

Printed by permission of Signpost Books, Ltd., England

First Canadian edition published 1994

Canadian Cataloguing in Publication Data

Granfield, Linda
      1987, the year I was born : a daily record of events

ISBN 1-55074-144-6

1. Nineteen eighty-seven, A.D. - Chronology - Juvenile literature.
2. Canada - History - 1963-- Chronology - Juvenile literature.*
I. Slavin, Bill.   II. Title.

FC630.G73 1994   j971.064'7   C93-095117-4
F1034.2.G73 1994

Kids Can Press Ltd.
29 Birch Avenue
Toronto, Ontario, Canada
M4V 1E2

Edited by Lori Burwash
Designed by Esperança Melo
Printed and bound in Hong Kong

94 0 9 8 7 6 5 4 3 2 1

A Week of Birthdays

Monday's child is fair of face,
Tuesday's child is full of grace,
Wednesday's child is full of woe,
Thursday's child has far to go,
Friday's child is loving and giving,
Saturday's child works hard for its living,
But the child that's born on the Sabbath day
Is bonny and blithe, and good and gay.

The Days of the Week

Sunday — the sun's day

Monday — the moon's day

Tuesday — day of Tiu, or Tyr, the Norse god of war and the sky

Wednesday — Woden's day (Woden, or Odin, was the chief Norse god)

Thursday — Thor's day (in Norse mythology, Thor was the god of thunder)

Friday — Freya's day (Freya was a wife of Odin and the goddess of love and beauty)

Saturday — Saturn's day (in Roman mythology, Saturn was a harvest god)

The Months

January — the month of Janus, Roman god of doorways, who had two faces looking in opposite directions

February — the month of februa, a Roman festival of purification

March — the month of Mars, the Roman god of war

April — the month of Venus, the Roman goddess of love

May — the month of Maia, the Roman goddess of spring

June — the month of Juno, the principal Roman goddess

July — the month of Roman emperor Julius Caesar

August — the month of Roman emperor Augustus

September — the seventh (*septem*) month of the old Roman calendar

October — the eighth (*octo*) month of the old Roman calendar

November — the ninth (*novem*) month of the old Roman calendar

December — the tenth (*decem*) month of the old Roman calendar

Birthstones and Flowers

January — garnet, snowdrop

February — amethyst, primrose

March — aquamarine, violet

April — diamond, daisy

May — emerald, hawthorn

June — moonstone, rose

July — ruby, water lily

August — peridot, poppy

September — sapphire, morning glory

October — opal, hops

November — topaz, chrysanthemum

December — turquoise, holly

Extra! Extra!

Gondolas Disappearing from Venice

The stately gondola — a symbol of Venice, Italy, for over 1000 years — is in danger. The few active master builders are nearing old age, and there is only a handful of young apprentices to continue making the beautiful 12-m-long boats. Each wooden boat takes one person two to three months to build.

Long ago, the city's 180 canals were filled with more than 10 000 gondolas, but motorized water buses and taxis have reduced the number to nearly 400. A special agency for gondolas and gondoliers (the boat operators) is trying to save the boats by proposing the establishment of a gondola school, where young students can learn how to make the boats and, later, become apprentices. A museum dedicated to the Venetian gondola is also planned.

Chinese New Year

For Chinese people around the world, New Year's Day is the most important celebration of the year. In the Chinese calendar, years are associated with one of 12 beasts: 1987 is the Year of the Rabbit, the luckiest of all the beast signs. People born in the Year of the Rabbit are, according to custom, affectionate yet shy, talented and well-spoken.

Many traditions are part of the New Year's celebration. Red is worn because it's considered a lucky colour, and children are given envelopes of "lucky money." Carefully prepared foods also represent good fortune in the year to come.

Trivia tidbit

In 1987, Canada had 119 newspapers with an average daily circulation of 5.8 million.

You said it!

"Don't let the cat out of the bag!" Long ago, dishonest sellers sometimes tricked customers by putting a cat into a bag, instead of meat. At home, the buyer discovered the switch. The expression has been used for over 600 years and still means "don't give away the secret."

What's *that*?!? Snowsnake

Nobody knows exactly when the Native game of Snowsnake began, but it is still played each winter by players who hurl greased hardwood sticks (snakes) down a sloping track in the snow. Snakes can be hurled more than 2 km and can reach speeds of 240 km/h. The team whose snake travels the farthest wins.

JANUARY

Thursday 1

New Year's Day

Frobisher Bay, Northwest Territories, changes its name to Iqaluit, which means "fish" in Inuktitut. It is the traditional Native name of the southeast area of Baffin Island, where the town is located.

Friday 2

Across Canada, Polar Bear Club members are thawing out after their annual New Year's swim. Halifax members braved Halifax Harbour's 2°C waters, but swimmers in Vancouver enjoyed English Bay's 8.3°C waters.

☆ **1932** — birth of Jean Little, author of *Hey World, Here I Am!*

Saturday 3

More than 1000 Canadians have signed a huge greeting card for imprisoned South African nationalist Nelson Mandela.

☆ **1939** — birth of Bobby Hull, hockey player

Sunday 4

After 19 months of touring the world by wheelchair to raise money for spinal cord research, Rick Hansen reaches Thunder Bay, Ontario, where he pays tribute to Terry Fox.

Monday 5

Fire destroys the Victoriaville Hockey Stick Inc. plant in Quebec. The company is one of the world's largest manufacturers of hockey sticks, producing 800 000 sticks a year. Only 100 000 sticks were saved.

Tuesday 6

Lawnmowers obsolete? Perhaps. Jan Weijer, a professor at the University of Alberta, has developed "supergrass," which requires little water and no fertilizer. The grass only needs to be cut once a year.

Wednesday 7

Publisher Mel Hurtig has announced plans to create a special encyclopedia of Canada for children 8 to 14 years old. The five-volume project will cost $10 million.

☆ **1827** — birth of Sir Sandford Fleming, inventor, scientist, railway surveyor and engineer

Thursday 8

Catcher Ernie Whitt signs a three-year, $2-million contract with the Toronto Blue Jays.

Friday 9

Canadian rock group Glass Tiger, composer David Foster and trombonist Rob McConnell have been nominated for Grammy Awards.

☆ **1802** — birth of Catharine Parr Traill, author of *The Backwoods of Canada*

Saturday 10

This year, for the first time, Soviet consumers will be able to buy Coca-Cola bottled in the Soviet Union.

☆ **1938** — birth of Frank Mahovlich, hockey player

Sunday 11

Astronomers have detected skylight from the birth of a galaxy 12 billion years ago. This new information disproves the Big Bang theory.

☆ **1815** — birth of Sir John A. Macdonald, first prime minister of Canada

☆ **1934** — birth of Jean Chrétien, 20th prime minister of Canada

JANUARY

Monday
12

In Calgary, cyclists are outside, zoo attendance is high, and people are sunbathing, as the temperature hits a record 17°C. Meanwhile, Ontario is digging out after a storm that dumped 15.2 cm of snow.

Tuesday
13

An Edmonton company has developed the Golden Hawk, an ultralight aircraft that can be made from a kit. The two-passenger plane uses regular gas and can land in a field.

Wednesday
14

What a catch! The Royal Ontario Museum needs a big freezer to exhibit a prehistoric coelacanth whose ancestors date back 325 million years. The 1.22-m, 27-kg fish was caught at the Comoro Islands off Africa and was donated to the ROM.
☆ **1855** — birth of Homer Watson, painter

Thursday
15

An Edmonton entrepreneur has developed a toothbrush that rinses your teeth while you brush. The Aqua Plus has a built-in mechanism that eliminates the need to gargle.
☆ **1947** — birth of Veronica Tennant, ballet dancer

Friday
16

Parishioners of the 800-year-old church in Burnam Thorpe, England, have invited the residents of Burnamthorpe Road in Etobicoke, Ontario, to help raise funds to save the historic building. Burnam Thorpe was the birthplace of Admiral Lord Nelson, a 19th-century British naval hero.
☆ **1948** — birth of Cliff Thorburn, champion snooker player

Saturday
17

Superstar Michael Jackson has signed a multimillion-dollar, multi-year deal to appear in new Pepsi commercials.
☆ **1929** — birth of Jacques Plante, hockey goaltender and the first goalie to wear a protective mask regularly

Sunday
18

The magnetic resonance imaging scanner has been announced. This new science tool uses radio waves and a magnetic field to see through bones and teeth. It can spot trouble in your head before you feel a headache!
☆ **1939** — birth of David French, playwright

Monday
19

The United Nations reports that the world's population will pass 5 billion by June 1987.
☆ **1934** — birth of Lloyd Robertson, T.V. anchor and reporter

Tuesday
20

Yo-Yo champ Al Gallo is coming out of retirement to promote the revival of the famous spinning toy. From 1938 to 1981, 1.5 million Yo-Yos sold every year in Canada.
☆ **1921** — birth of Jacques Ferron, a doctor and the founder of the Rhinoceros Party

JANUARY

Wednesday 21
Mickey Mouse visits Parliament Hill and makes House of Commons Speaker John Fraser an honorary citizen of Walt Disney World.
☆ **1937** — birth of Jim Unger, cartoonist and creator of "Herman"

Thursday 22
Singer Aretha Franklin has become the first woman voted into the Rock and Roll Hall of Fame.

Friday 23
John Rubick of Welland, Ontario, has 1700 licence plates in his garage. They include bear-shaped plates and commemorative licence plates from U.S. inaugurations and the Pope's visit to Canada.
☆ **1929** — birth of John Polanyi, professor and co-winner of a Nobel Prize for Chemistry

Saturday 24
The Snowsnake contest at the Six Nations Reserve in Ontario kicks off a season of matches.

Sunday 25
It's Super Bowl XXI — the New York Giants defeat the Denver Broncos 39–20.

Monday 26
The Victorian Order of Nurses celebrates 90 years of at-home nursing service in Canada.
☆ **1961** — birth of Wayne Gretzky, hockey player

Tuesday 27
Colonel Sheila Hellstrom is named the first female general in the history of the Canadian Armed Forces.
☆ **1953** — birth of Frank Augustyn, ballet dancer

Wednesday 28
Electronic babysitters are the hot new Canadian product. The battery-operated, two-piece alarm system includes a part to attach to the child's clothing and another part for the adult. When the child wanders off, the alarm sounds.
☆ **1822** — birth of Alexander Mackenzie, second prime minister of Canada

Thursday 29
Chinese New Year
It's New Year's Day for Chinese people around the world. Kung Hay Fatt Choy!

Friday 30
INs and OUTs for 1987 are already listed. OUTs include Trivial Pursuit, designer-label clothes, Sylvester Stallone and high-impact aerobics. INs include Twister, acid-washed denim, Arnold Schwarzenegger and bowling.

Saturday 31
A 322-km section of the South Nahanni River in the Northwest Territories has been proclaimed a Canadian Heritage River.
☆ **1928** — birth of Gathie Falk, multimedia artist

FEBRUARY

Extra! Extra!

Secret Admirer Sends 60th Valentine

Meryl Dunsmore is 76 years old and is still puzzled and pleased by the secret admirer who has been sending her valentines since she was a high-school student. The cards have been sent from different places around the world, and the sender has always known Dunsmore's address, even though she's moved at least six times. This year's card, Cupid shooting his arrow through three hearts, arrived from Melbourne, Australia, in a red envelope.

Valentine's Day

Valentine's Day is one of the oldest card-sending occasions, but no one is sure how it began. One possibility is ancient Rome's festival of Lupercalia. Young women wrote love messages and put them into an urn, and each young man drew a message from the urn. He courted the woman whose name he picked for the rest of the year. Cupid was a part of the festival's symbolism.

Valentine cards, as we know them, were first printed nearly 200 years ago in Europe and have been available in North America for the last 150 years. Covered with lace, hearts and skilful artwork, valentines carry serious or humorous expressions of friendship and love.

Trivia tidbit
Canadians bought 60 million valentines in 1987.

What's *that*?!? Philtrum
The indentation under your nose and above your upper lip is called a philtrum. The same word also means "love potion."

You said it!
"You're the cat's pyjamas."
The 1920s, or Roaring Twenties, gave us this expression referring to total excellence. "Cat's meow" and "cat's whiskers" were similar expressions that became trendy compliments when they were used to describe the popular 1920s actress Clara Bow.

Sunday 1
Hollywood is 100! A special Oscar statuette is put into a time capsule.
☆ **1882** — birth of Louis St. Laurent, 12th prime minister of Canada

Monday 2
Groundhog Day
Wiarton Willie, Ontario's legendary groundhog, predicts an early spring. Harold Silk, mayor of Wiarton, says Willie saw no shadow: "He would need a flashlight to find his way around, it was so dark."

Tuesday 3
Ferguson Jenkins has been named to the Canadian Baseball Hall of Fame. The right-handed pitcher won 284 games during 19 seasons in the major leagues.
☆ **1843** — birth of Sir William Van Horne, railway official

FEBRUARY

Wednesday
4
Thirty moose will be airlifted by helicopter from Ontario's Algonquin Provincial Park and sent to Michigan to increase the state's moose population.

Thursday
5
Cross-country skiing, the world's oldest winter sport, is changing. A side-to-side motion has become a new style, called snow skating.

Friday
6
Montreal wakes up to read its newest and fifth daily newspaper, *Le Matin*.

Saturday
7
Swimmer Victor Davis of Waterloo, Ontario, sets a new world short-course record in the men's 200-m breaststroke in Bonn, Germany.
☆ **1945** — birth of Colette Whiten, sculptor

Sunday
8
Warmly dressed residents of Richmond Hill, Ontario, race unmade beds across Mill Pond during the annual Richmond Hill Carnival Bedrace.

Monday
9
A new fashion fad has arrived from Europe — designer eyeglasses for kids.
☆ **1894** — birth of Billy Bishop, World War I pilot

Tuesday
10
The 100th birthday of the Royal Conservatory of Music in Toronto.
☆ **1955** — birth of Brenda Clark, illustrator of *Franklin Fibs*

Wednesday
11
Forty years ago this week the Alberta oil-and-gas industry roared to life with the spouting of the historic Imperial Leduc Number 1 well.

Thursday
12
Academy Award nominations are announced. Five Canadians are Oscar contenders in the best song, make-up and feature film categories.
☆ **1959** — birth of Bill Slavin, the illustrator of this book

Friday
13
Rendez-Vous '87, in Quebec City, has ended in a draw. The Canadian hockey team (Team NHL) won the first game 4–3, and the Soviet national hockey team won the second game 5–3.
☆ **1925** — birth of Gerald Tailfeathers, one of the first Native Canadians to become a professional artist

Saturday
14
Valentine's Day
Fitness programs for flabby tots are a new fitness trend. Children and their parents work out through games that develop motor skills and rhythm.

Sunday
15
Vanessa Harwood dances her last performance as a principal dancer with the National Ballet.

Monday
16
St John's, Newfoundland, is digging out from a record one-day, 47-cm snowfall.

Tuesday
17
Newspaper misprint?? The *Toronto Star* reports: "A record 16.2 tourists visited Canada last year, up 18 per cent from 1985." Watch out for similar crowds this year!
☆ **1820** — birth of Elzéar-Alexandre Taschereau, first Canadian cardinal

FEBRUARY

Wednesday 18
Canadian children's entertainer Raffi, on his first major U.S. tour, is a hit. Concerts are sold out in every city, and record sales are over 100 000.
☆ **1916** — birth of Jean Drapeau, mayor of Montreal during the 1967 World Expo and the 1976 Summer Olympics

Thursday 19
Tennis superstar Bjorn Borg launches a new men's fragrance in Toronto. Called "Bjorn Borg," the product comes in a bottle shaped like the grip of a tennis racket.

Friday 20
Doctors have reported a case of "joystick digit," caused by moving the joystick of video games for hours. Even after being unlocked, the finger can bend back into a locked position.
☆ **1942** — birth of Phil Esposito, hockey player

Saturday 21
Computer failure costs Calgary's Jim Read the winning position at the Canadian super giant slalom championships at Mont Ste-Anne, Quebec. When the race was hand-timed, Alain Villiard of Quebec was named the winner.

Sunday 22
There's plenty of police aid available in the Crawford family of Toronto. Five members of the family have worked or are working in various police departments.
☆ **1903** — birth of Morley Callaghan, novelist

Monday 23
The University of Toronto's Ian Shelton spots a massive super-nova — the brightest celestial explosion seen from Earth in 382 years — from U of T's southern observatory in Chile's Andes mountains.

Tuesday 24
Grammy Award night: Glass Tiger and Rob McConnell miss out on awards, but David Foster wins.
☆ **1866** — birth of Martha Black, Yukon naturalist and second woman elected to Parliament

Wednesday 25
Rudolf Nureyev is a guest dancer at the National Ballet of Canada's celebration of its 35th anniversary.

Thursday 26
Designer toilet seats? An advertisement announces a selection of 20 colours with soft foam stuffing — for your sitting pleasure!
☆ **1961** — birth of Vicki Keith, marathon swimmer

Friday 27
Five generations of females in an Ajax, Ontario, family get together to celebrate the birth of six-day-old Elisha Danielle Neal.
☆ **1899** — birth of Charles Best, co-discoverer of insulin

Saturday 28
Bridget Kimmons has a lot of ups and downs in her job; she works one of the few manually operated elevators left in Toronto. The 1907 model has only been stuck three or four times in Bridget's 12 years on the job.
☆ **1712** — birth of Louis-Joseph Montcalm, military leader

MARCH

Extra! Extra!

Toad Tunnel Aims to Save Thousands

In an effort to save the 150 000 amphibians squashed under cars each year, Britain has opened its first toad tunnel. Built under a road in Hambleden, 80 km west of London, the tunnel follows the toads' migration path to the spawning pond.

According to experts, about 10 000 toads cross the road during a five-day period in early March, the peak migration season. The toads are channelled to the tunnel by a 30-cm-high plastic fence. The fence runs for several hundred metres through the woods to the crossing.

Before the tunnel was built, volunteers ferried the toads across the road in buckets each evening, and toad road mortality was about 20 t a year. The new tunnel will help reduce the number of car accidents caused by skidding.

Academy Awards 1987

Millions of viewers around the world watched the film industry celebrate Oscar Night, the evening of the Academy Awards. The major awards were:

☆ Best Actor — Paul Newman, in *The Color of Money*
☆ Best Actress — Marlee Matlin, in *Children of a Lesser God*
☆ Best Picture — *Platoon*

Trivia tidbit
The 1987 Metropolitan Toronto telephone books used 93.5 t of ink, 5928 t of white paper, 75 t of blue paper and 36 t of glue — 2 million telephone books were printed.

What's *that* ?!?   *Taiko*
Taiko is the Japanese word for a special variety of drums. These drums come in many sizes, from hand drums to large mounted wooden drums such as *O-daiko*, which is 1.5 m across. Another of the drums is made from an entire cow skin stretched across a tree trunk!

You said it!
"Get off your high horse!"

In the 1300s, royalty and other nobles rode tall horses during pageants and processions. These high mounts became symbols of the riders' superiority. Ever since, the expression has been used to tell somebody to stop behaving as if he or she were better than everybody else.

MARCH

Sunday
1
Edmontonian Art Boileau wins the Los Angeles Marathon, beating 15 000 other runners to the finish line in the 42.1-km race.
☆ 1947 — birth of Alan Thicke, actor

Monday
2
Waiter, there's a flower in my salad! Canadians are enjoying pansy, rose and marigold petals in salads served in fashionable restaurants.
☆ 1948 — birth of Camilla Gryski, author of *Cat's Cradle, Owl's Eyes: A Book of String Games*

Tuesday
3
Harry Levinson of Markham, Ontario, has 20 000 bubble-gum cards in his growing collection. The card junkie's favourites include cards from the old T.V. shows "The Munsters," "Leave It to Beaver" and "Batman."
☆ 1847 — birth of Alexander Graham Bell, inventor of the telephone

Wednesday
4
Severe knee injuries force Canadian World Cup downhill skier Todd Brooker into early retirement at the age of 27.
☆ 1901 — birth of Wilbur Franks, inventor of the "G suit," which was later refined for astronauts

Thursday
5
Popular actors Tom Selleck and Ted Danson prepare to film the movie *Three Men and a Baby* in Ontario. The search begins for two sets of twin girls to share the baby role.

Friday
6
Japan's Kodo drummers, on their One Earth tour, perform in Toronto. Eleven players beat rhythms on dozens of *taiko*. The drummers must apprentice for a year in order to play the thundering drums. (*Kodo* means "heartbeat" and "children of the drum.")
☆ 1940 — birth of Ken Danby, artist

Saturday
7
In Vatican City, Italy, a Metis delegation from Alberta has given Pope John Paul II the name "Chief Holy White Father" and a pair of handmade moosehide moccasins.

Sunday
8
International Women's Day
Ah, fresh air! Scientists in Egypt prepare to use space technology to analyse the ancient air in a pit sealed 4600 years ago.

Monday
9
Jan, a performing elephant in the Shrine Circus, gets her nails polished before a show in Toronto.

Tuesday
10
Who is calling? People are warned that automated telephone sales "people," with computer-generated or taped voices, are being used more and more.
☆ 1947 — birth of Kim Campbell, 19th, and first woman, prime minister of Canada

MARCH

Wednesday
11

The search continues for Great Canadian Dogs. Canada's 2.7 million dog owners have the chance to win a $10 000 cash prize and to see their pet become a national celebrity.
☆ **1943** — birth of Sharon Siamon, author of *Fishing for Trouble*

Thursday
12

Brian Orser wins a gold medal at the world figure skating championships in Cincinnati, Ohio. Fans wave a 3.5-m-long banner covered with 1000 signatures from people in Orillia, Ontario, where he lives.
☆ **1821** — birth of Sir John Abbott, third prime minister of Canada

Friday
13

Statistics Canada reports that more than 1 million Canadians travelled out of the country in January, and most went in search of sun and sand. Meanwhile, nearly 1.5 million visitors came to Canada … for the cold and snow?
☆ **1914** — birth of W.O. Mitchell, author of *Who Has Seen the Wind*

Saturday
14

Book now! A Vancouver travel company is organizing a Concorde flight that will travel 17 km above Earth. From that amazing height, passengers will see the globe's curvature against the blackness of space. Cost for the two-hour flight: $895 per person.
☆ **1932** — birth of Norval Morrisseau, Ojibwa artist

Sunday
15

Purim
In Edmonton, wheelchair athlete Rick Hansen sets out on the Yellowhead Highway and begins his push to the Rocky Mountains.
☆ **1943** — birth of David Cronenberg, film maker

Monday
16

A Montreal university's study shows that the human body can absorb the calcium in chocolate milk just as easily as that in white milk. Kids cheer … and order *double* chocolate milk.
☆ **1934** — birth of Ramon Hnatyshyn, 24th governor general of Canada

Tuesday
17

St Patrick's Day
Bell Canada announces its "heftiest ever" Metropolitan Toronto phone book: 1991 pages filled with over a million phone numbers.

Wednesday
18

Ontario has an egg problem. Consumers buy up all the large eggs, and stores run out. Manitoba has extras, but shipping is too eggs-pensive.
☆ **1869** — birth of Maude Abbott, an acclaimed pathologist barred from medicine because she was a woman

Thursday
19

Welwyn Wilton Katz, of London, Ontario, beats 150 entries and wins the first International Children's Fiction contest for her novel *False Face*.

Friday
20

Spring Equinox
Rick Hansen is back in British Columbia, where he started the Man in Motion tour around the world two years ago.
☆ **1939** — birth of Brian Mulroney, 18th prime minister of Canada

MARCH

Saturday 21
Author Robert Munsch admits to reporters at a car show that he'd like to sell "a few million more books" and buy a Mercedes — but he has a new baby, so he's shopping for a van.

Sunday 22
Known as Spike on the T.V. show "Degrassi Junior High," 16-year-old Amanda Steptoe gives a tour of her bedroom. The walls are papered with about 150 photos of her favourite rock stars, including Billy Idol, Duran Duran and Platinum Blonde.
☆ **1909** — birth of Gabrielle Roy, author of *My Cow Bossie*

Monday 23
Nova Scotia sailor John Hughes tells how he did what no lone sailor has done before — sailed a boat with a broken mast around treacherous Cape Horn, on the southern tip of South America. After bouncing on the ocean for 64 days, he reached the Falkland Islands safely.

Tuesday 24
A building company in Bowmanville, Ontario, gives new meaning to "home delivery." It will deliver a pre-packaged house within an hour of receiving an order. If the foundation is already in place, the home can be built in one day.
☆ **1936** — birth of David Suzuki, geneticist and broadcaster

Wednesday 25
A m-o-o-o-ving experience in Hampshire, Prince Edward Island. Elizabeth Ward finds the kitchen tap dry; her husband finds their 544-kg steer in the well. It takes seven men three hours to get the animal out.

Thursday 26
Rock-solid protection: The newest deodorant in Canada is a white crystal stone imported from France. It is free of perfume and chemicals, and when rubbed on the skin, the wet stone leaves an invisible mineral-salt deposit that prevents bacteria.
☆ **1951** — birth of Martin Short, actor and comedian

Friday 27
Ford Canada demonstrates its new inflatable air bags, which are designed for passenger safety.

Saturday 28
For the fourth year in a row, Canadian women are the world's best at curling. This year's women's world curling championships were held in Chicago, Illinois.
☆ **1951** — birth of Karen Kain, dancer

Sunday 29
The 23rd annual Maple Syrup Festival continues in Elmira, Ontario. Local farmer John Weber gathers sap the old-fashioned way — in metal buckets. Two men make rounds 18 times a day to empty the buckets on 1900 trees.
☆ **1927** — birth of Donn Kushner, author of *A Book Dragon*

Monday 30
Academy Award night in Los Angeles, California: Canadian Oscar winners are Brigitte Berman (best documentary) and David Cronenberg's *The Fly* (best make-up).

Tuesday 31
The skeleton of a fin whale is on display at Science North in Sudbury, Ontario. Discovered in the early 1980s at Anticosti Island, in the Gulf of St Lawrence, the whale measures 23 m and extends through two levels of the museum.
☆ **1950** — birth of Ian Wallace, author-illustrator of *Morgan the Magnificent*

APRIL

Extra! Extra!

Clothes-dryer Garbage Becomes Art

Some people receive greeting cards in the mail, but California artist Slater Barron gets envelopes filled with lint. Her friends even go door-to-door to collect lint for her stockpile! Barron is a well-known lint artist. She uses coloured lint from vacuum cleaners and clothes dryers to make large portraits and models of rooms that are nearly life-sized. She keeps the lint sorted by colour — just like an artist's palette — in her studio.

People are surprised to find out that each piece of art is made with recycled materials. Some of the lint has bits of hair, ticket stubs, grass, wire or clothing labels that went through the wash cycle — tiny bits of people's lives that have become art.

Barron's latest project is a frog sculpture. She is using a dried frog carcass as her model.

Commercial Characters

The chubby, giggly Pillsbury Doughboy won a popularity contest sponsored by the magazine *Advertising Age*. Readers were asked to choose their favourite commercial characters. Other favourites included Morris the Cat, the Keebler Elves, Life Cereal's Mikey, Ronald McDonald, Tony the Tiger, the Snuggle Bear and the California Raisins.

Trivia tidbit

The new roof of Montreal's Olympic Stadium is made of 18 580 m² of orange canvas, fabric and steel. It weighs 165 t.

You said it!

"I'll be there in two shakes of a lamb's tail!" Lambs are playful and always move quickly. For at least 150 years, the expression has been used to mean "very soon" or "very quickly."

What's *that*?!? Pysanka

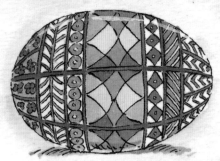

Ukrainian Easter celebrations include the *pysanka*, or traditional Easter egg. The *pysanka* is decorated with a bright design and given to a special friend as a good-luck symbol. This tradition is thousands of years old.

APRIL

Wednesday 1

April Fool's Day
Halifax Harbour, proudly called the world's ice-free port, shuts down for the first time in living memory due to a freak ice build-up.

Thursday 2

Rick Hansen reaches his home town of Williams Lake, British Columbia. After a quick family visit, the "man in motion" begins the final leg of his journey around the world.

Friday 3

What a photo album! The Public Archives of Canada has acquired the lifetime collection of Canadian photographer Yousuf Karsh. The collection includes over 60 000 prints and transparencies spanning 60 years.

Saturday 4

Time to spring ahead. Daylight saving time begins, and in Ontario, clock repairman Frank Thornton moves forward the hands on more than 60 clocks in his shop.
☆ **1940** — birth of Phoebe Gilman, author of *Something from Nothing*

Sunday 5

In Vancouver, the Canadian men's team beats the West German team 9–5 and wins the men's world curling championship.

Monday 6

Vincent van Gogh's 1888 masterpiece, *Sunflowers*, has sold for $51.9 million, four times the world-record price for an auctioned painting.

Tuesday 7

More than 1000 Calgary kids gather for the first rehearsal of the five-minute routine they'll perform at the opening ceremonies of the Winter Olympics in February 1988.
☆ **1851** — birth of John Bengough, political cartoonist

Wednesday 8

Fashion designer Alfred Sung unveils new uniforms for Canada's Girl Guides. The outfits are more comfortable and are made with natural-fibre fabrics — just what the Guides wanted!

Thursday 9

Ten Canadian veterans of the Battle of Vimy Ridge meet on the battle site in France to mark the 70th anniversary of Canada's greatest military victory.

Friday 10

Double-dipped? Chocolate-covered potato chips are available in Canada. The gourmet treat costs $20 for a 0.5-kg container.

Saturday 11

New Canadian stamps, issued to publicize the 1988 Winter Olympics in Calgary, feature speed skating and bobsleigh racing.
☆ **1914** — birth of Norman McLaren, director of animated films

APRIL

Sunday 12
After 11 years and millions of dollars, Montreal's Olympic Stadium finally has a roof.

Monday 13
The Mikado is the longest-running Canadian production on Broadway (New York) — and it's going to be around even longer. It will play for at least five weeks, instead of three.

Tuesday 14
Passover begins
"Max Headroom," a new comedy/adventure T.V. series, features Canadian actor Matt Frewer as Max, a computer-generated talking head.

Wednesday 15
Canadians who want to carry the Olympic torch for some of its cross-country trip to Calgary in 1988 have mailed in more than 6.6 million applications. Organizers, expecting only 250 000 applications, are stunned — and happy!

Thursday 16
Madame Justice Claire L'Heureux-Dubé, of Quebec, has become the second woman to be appointed to the 112-year-old Supreme Court of Canada.
☆ **1907** — birth of J. Armand Bombardier, inventor of the snowmobile

Friday 17
Northern Dancer, called the world's greatest living stallion, has retired from the fathering business. The 26-year-old racehorse has sired offspring, including 124 race winners, since 1965.
☆ **1620** — birth of Marguerite Bourgeoys, canonized founder of the Congrégation de Notre-Dame de Montréal

Saturday 18
Airport customs officials in Canada confess they've seen everything: live birds hidden under a coat, a boa constrictor wrapped around someone's waist and salamis in shoes — that were on someone's feet. Ouch!
☆ **1953** — birth of Rick Moranis, actor

Sunday 19
Easter
Ten centimetres of snow make it hard to find eggs at the Calgary Zoo's annual Easter egg hunt. Meanwhile, Easter paraders in Toronto are wearing bathing suits and shorts, and the temperature rises to 23°C.

Monday 20
Canadians are collecting anything they can find from the 1950s — clothing, jewellery, coloured aluminum tumblers, plastic (Melmac) dishes and boomerang-shaped tables.
☆ **1949** — birth of Toller Cranston, figure skater and artist

Tuesday 21
In Montreal, more than 50 000 baseball fans watch the first Expos home game played under a roof.
☆ **1841** — birth of Jennie Kidd Trout, the first Canadian woman licensed to practise medicine in Canada

APRIL

Wednesday 22
Earth Day
In England, Vancouver athlete Paul Dolan plays his first game as goalkeeper for the English soccer team Third Division Notts County. The team dates back to 1888.
☆ 1952 — birth of Kathy Stinson, author of *Red is Best*

Thursday 23
Shinji Kazama has become the first person to reach the North Pole by motorcycle. The 780-km trek from Ward Hunt Island took 47 days. Kazama's motorcycle had a ski in place of its front wheel.
☆ 1897 — birth of Lester Pearson, 14th prime minister of Canada

Friday 24
Popular movies currently playing are *Project X*, Disney's *The Aristocats*, *Raising Arizona* and *Crocodile Dundee*.

Saturday 25
Statistics Canada reports that the average Canadian watches 24.2 hours of television a week. Only 8.7 minutes of that time are spent watching educational programs. Newfoundlanders watch the most T.V. (27 hours); Albertans watch the least (22.2 hours).

Sunday 26
Canada's song-and-dance man, Jeff Hyslop, is ready to open in *The Fabulous Kelley* at Young People's Theatre in Toronto. The musical is based on Dr Thomas P. Kelley, an entertainer and businessman who lived in Nova Scotia around 1900.
☆ 1922 — birth of Jeanne Sauvé, the first woman to be appointed governor general of Canada

Monday 27
The Canada Council announces its Children's Literature prizes. The winners include: Janet Lunn (author of *Shadow in Hawthorn Bay*), Raymond Plante (author of *Le Dernier des Raisons*), Barbara Reid (illustrator of *Have You Seen Birds?*) and Stephane Poulin (illustrator of *As-tu vu Josephine?* and *Album de Famille*).
☆ 1954 — birth of Jan Hudson, author of *Sweetgrass*

Tuesday 28
The jugglers, clowns and high-wire artists of Quebec's Le Cirque du Soleil have been invited to the Los Angeles Festival this autumn. It will be the group's first U.S. appearance.
☆ 1935 — birth of Robert "Bob" White, labour leader

Wednesday 29
Robin Seal, 10, and Jason Westwood, 9, of Ganonoque, Ontario, discover a winning lottery ticket while searching through a trash bin for pop bottles. The money ($25 000) is theirs to keep. They plan to buy bikes but will invest the rest of the loot.

Thursday 30
Fashion is a hot topic at a food-services convention in Toronto. Plastic gloves and beard nets are a must, but only the top cook in a kitchen can wear the tallest hat, which is 38 cm high.
☆ 1947 — birth of Kit Pearson, author of *The Sky is Falling*

MAY

Extra! Extra!

Rick Hansen Crosses the Finish Line

Wheelchair athlete Rick Hansen reached the finish line of his Man in Motion tour on May 22. It was day 792 of the around-the-world journey to promote awareness of spinal cord injuries. Only 300 people had gathered at a Vancouver mall to see him off on March 21, 1985, but over 10 000 cheering fans welcomed him home. Hansen, 29, raised more than $15 million for research, pushed his wheelchair wheels more than 16 million times, toured 34 countries and travelled over 40 000 km. He's looking forward to a long rest!

Wearing the Blues

Blue jeans have been around for a long time, but now there are new versions of the old classic. "Abused" denim looks beat up or worn, "destroyed" denim looks like old leather and "stone-aged" denim is a lighter blue than a regular blue jean. But "mud wash" is the most popular look: jeans are acid-washed with an overdye of khaki green or dirt brown.

Trivia tidbit
Toronto's Name the Dome contest ran for one month: 150 000 entries were received, and 12 879 different names were suggested. Two thousand people sent the name "SkyDome."

You said it!
"You're eagle-eyed."

Eagles have exceptional eyesight. So if someone is eagle-eyed, it means he or she is good at seeing small things or things that are far away.

What's *that*?!?   Snowdome

Souvenir hounds have collected snowdomes for more than 100 years. A snowdome is a clear plastic or glass dome filled with water, a scene and "snow" — pieces of wax, clay or ground rice. Snowdomes are also called snowies or shakies.

MAY

Friday
1

Carolyn Waldo and Michelle Cameron win at the Canadian synchronized swimming championships in Etobicoke, Ontario.
☆ **1831** — birth of Emily Stowe, the first Canadian woman to practise medicine in Canada

Saturday
2

Ontario's Polar Bear Provincial Park includes the world's most southerly tundra. Located where James Bay meets Hudson Bay, the park is home to arctic fox, caribou and polar bears.

Sunday
3

Buddhist leaders announce the discovery of two gold bowls in a cave near Beijing, China. The bowls, from A.D. 616, contained bone fragments believed to be from the body of Buddha.
☆ **1947** — birth of Doug Henning, magician

Monday
4

China agrees to loan two giant pandas to the Calgary Zoo. Construction of a special exhibit to house the pandas starts immediately.
☆ **1929** — birth of Eric Wright, mystery writer

Tuesday
5

Canadian Steve Fonyo, who lost a leg to cancer, finishes his 1400-km Journey for Lives run through Scotland and England. The three-month trek raised money for cancer research in Great Britain.
☆ **1843** — birth of William Beers, a dentist who campaigned to have lacrosse accepted as Canada's national game

Wednesday
6

New food products being test-marketed include vegetable ice creams, Cherry 7-Up, fish sausages and "chewy chalk," bubble gum that looks just like real blackboard chalk!

Thursday
7

Rick Hansen is east of Penticton, British Columbia, and about 400 km away from Vancouver and the end of the Man in Motion tour.

Friday
8

In Vatican City, Italy, Pope John Paul II announces his plans to visit Fort Simpson, Northwest Territories, and Batoche, Saskatchewan, next summer.

Saturday
9

Super pen-pal Barbara Wooley, of Red Deer, Alberta, writes six letters a day, seven days a week — and receives about as many from her friends around the world. That's a lot of letters!
☆ **1928** — birth of Barbara Ann Scott, Olympic figure skating champion

Sunday
10

In Rome, 1500 pilgrims from Canada attend the ceremony that brings Quebec's Bishop Louis-Zepherin Moreau (1824–1901) one step closer to sainthood.
☆ **1958** — birth of Gaetan Boucher, Olympic speed skater

Monday
11

SkyDome, Toronto's new domed stadium, is officially named. Kellie Watson, of Wallaceburg, Ontario, won the Name the Dome contest. She receives two tickets for life to every event held under the retractable roof.
☆ **1943** — birth of Nancy Greene, Olympic alpine skier

MAY

Tuesday
12
Gymnast Lori Strong has been named athlete of the month by the Sports Federation of Canada. One of her moves on the uneven parallel bars is so unique that officials may name it the Strong move and credit Lori as the inventor.
☆ **1921** — birth of Farley Mowat, author of *Lost in the Barrens*

Wednesday
13
Fabulous fungus! Genevieve de Rosemond's mushrooms have won her a place in the Canada-wide Science Fair at the University of Toronto. And they may also make her rich. The Albertan's supplies cost $3.50, but her gourmet crop would sell in a store for $250.00.
☆ **1904** — birth of Earle Birney, poet

Thursday
14
Denim still delights! New denim fashions feature fleece-collared jackets, short skirts trimmed in leather and zippers up the *back* of jeans.

Friday
15
Toronto schoolchildren help painter A.J. Casson celebrate the beginning of his 90th year, two days early. Casson is the last surviving member of the Group of Seven.

Saturday
16
Fergus, Ontario, calls itself the Teddy Bear Capital of the World. That's because Lee Wansbrough lives there — along with his 300 teddy bears and more than 100 bear-related items!

Sunday
17
Electronic bulletin boards are hot items. The boards post information, much like regular bulletin boards, except that people get the information over telephone lines and see it on their own computers. Police departments are using them already for some of their programs.
☆ **1898** — birth of A.J. Casson, painter and member of the Group of Seven

Monday
18
Victoria Day
British Columbia's lighthouse keepers send out an alert. They're upset because the government plans to replace them with automated lighthouses. Only 266 of Canada's original 600 lighthouses remain; 75 are already automated.
☆ **1957** — birth of Sharon Wood, the first woman from the Western Hemisphere to climb Mount Everest

Tuesday
19
The Fuller Brush Company celebrates 81 years of business in Canada. Some of the 2.5 million combs made by the company each year are photographed ... Say "Cheese!"
☆ **1952** — birth of Sarah Ellis, author of *Pick-Up Sticks*

Wednesday
20
In Halifax, people are trying to find a non-sexist term for "fishermen," and it's tough work. "Fisherpeople" isn't catching on, so "fishers" and "fisherfolk" are being considered.

MAY

Thursday 21
Roberta Bondar, Canada's first woman astronaut, tells 800 female students in Toronto to have a dream in life and to strive for it. She says the jobs of the future will be in science, and students shouldn't close any doors.
☆ **1928** — birth of Adele Wiseman, author

Friday 22
Rick Hansen reaches the finish line in Vancouver. It took him more than two years to complete his Man in Motion tour.

Saturday 23
He's not done yet! Wheelchair athlete Rick Hansen is honoured at B.C. Place, in Vancouver.

Sunday 24
Actress Paula Gallivan has been playing Elephant (Sharon, Lois and Bram's friend) for years — and it's been a pain in the neck. But not any longer! The 8.2-kg head has been rebuilt with braces that keep the weight off Paula's neck.
☆ **1930** — birth of Robert Bateman, painter

Monday 25
Anne of Avonlea, the sequel to *Anne of Green Gables*, is taking the U.S. by storm. With a Canadian story, author, producer, director and cast, the film is an all-Canadian export.
☆ **1879** — birth of Max Aitken (Lord Beaverbrook), politician and publisher

Tuesday 26
Gift-basket companies are popping up everywhere. A basket is filled with goodies, wrapped in shiny paper and ribbons, then delivered to some lucky kid.
☆ **1938** — birth of Teresa Stratas, opera singer

Wednesday 27
Divers give up their search for a prized baseball that was tossed into Lake Ontario after being stolen from the Canadian Baseball Hall of Fame. The ball is priceless because Babe Ruth hit it during a baseball game in Toronto in 1914.
☆ **1945** — birth of Bruce Cockburn, singer

Thursday 28
Halifax sailor John Hughes has finally finished his globe-circling voyage. He was the only Canadian — and the last of 16 sailors — to complete the trip, which began August 30, 1986.
☆ **1947** — birth of Lynn Johnston, cartoonist and creator of "For Better or For Worse"

Friday 29
Cabbage Patch Kids can now speak! Digitized speech technology and sensors in the dolls make them respond to touch and sound by talking. (But can they say "digitized speech technology"?)

Saturday 30
On-stage bloopers! Reporters ask actors what they do if they have to go to the bathroom or burp while on stage. Answers: The actors wet their pants, or they apologize to the audience after a big burp or sneeze. Of course, it helps if the play is a comedy.

Sunday 31
The Edmonton Oilers win the Stanley Cup by defeating the Philadelphia Flyers 3–1.

JUNE

Extra! Extra!

A New Coin for Canada

By July 1, 300 million one-dollar coins, called loonies, will be in circulation across Canada. The new coin has 11 sides and is slightly heavier and larger than a quarter. It will replace the dollar bill, which will be phased out by the end of 1989.

The story of the loonie began in 1978, when the Royal Canadian Mint sponsored a coin-design contest. A design featuring a voyageur was named the winner, and the coin dies were made. But the dies were lost by a courier service, and, for fear of forgery, the design had to be changed. Goodbye voyageur, hello loon.

The loon motif that is now on many one-dollar coins was designed by Bob Carmichael, who lives near Sault Ste Marie, Ontario. His design had placed second in the original contest ... sometimes even "final" decisions can change, and a runner-up can become a winner!

CASBY Awards 1987

♪ Best album: *Small Victories*, The Parachute Club
♪ Best group: The Parachute Club
♪ Best female vocalist: Luba
♪ Best male vocalist: Corey Hart
♪ Most promising group: The Pursuit of Happiness
♪ Most promising artist: Colin James
♪ Best single: "How Many (Rivers to Cross)," Luba
♪ Best international album: *Graceland*, Paul Simon
♪ Best video: "Dirty Water," Rock and Hyde
♪ Best jazz recording: *Streetnicks*, The Shuffle Demons

Trivia tidbit

In 1987, Canadians made over 37 billion telephone calls. Hello, hello ...

What's *that*?!?   Flin Flon

Flin Flon is a zinc- and copper-mining town in Manitoba. The town's name is believed to come from the book character Professor Josiah **Flin**tabbatey **Flon**atin, the adventurer-hero of *The Sunless City*, by J.E.P. Murdock, published in 1905.

You said it!

"It's raining cats and dogs."

In ancient mythology, people believed cats could influence the weather, particularly the rain. Dogs were associated with wild winds. So a windy rainstorm was called a cat-and-dog storm.

JUNE

Monday 1
Oatmeal has always been nutritious, but now it's trendy, too! Health-conscious people are gobbling up anything made with oat bran.

Tuesday 2
So long, Diane. Welcome, Rebecca. After five years on the popular television comedy "Cheers," Shelley Long is leaving, and Kirstie Alley will arrive as Rebecca Howe, the new manager.

Wednesday 3
Quebec premier Robert Bourassa is the last provincial leader to sign the Meech Lake Accord; it's the first time there is interprovincial harmony since 1981.
☆ 1926 — birth of Colleen Dewhurst, stage, film and television actress

Thursday 4
The Queen Mother begins a four-day visit to Montreal and is the first member of the royal family to visit Quebec in 11 years.

Friday 5
Rock star Bryan Adams headlines the Prince's Trust charity pop concerts in London and rehearses with Beatles Ringo Starr and George Harrison.
☆ 1939 — birth of Joe Clark, 16th prime minister of Canada

Saturday 6
Martians land at Toronto's CN Tower! Students from across Canada present 3-D models of aliens that could survive the dust storms, ultraviolet rays and low temperatures of the Red Planet.
☆ 1935 — birth of Joy Kogawa, author of *Naomi's Road*

Sunday 7
Canadians unhappy with the political scene met in Vancouver this week and formed a new party, the Reform Association of Canada.
☆ 1929 — birth of John Turner, 17th prime minister of Canada

Monday 8
In Toronto, the city health department launches Canada's first city-run AIDS hotline — and gets 156 calls in the first few hours.
☆ 1926 — birth of Elizabeth II, queen of Great Britain

Tuesday 9
Ontario hockey player Justine Blainey, with the help of a team of lawyers, presents two hours of testimony for the right to play hockey on a boys team.

Wednesday 10
Skipping rope will burn about 540 calories an hour, but double-dutch (skipping with two ropes) will burn more than 1000. Get your ropes ready!
☆ 1637 — birth of Father Jacques Marquette, missionary and co-discoverer of the Mississippi River

Thursday 11
Voters in Great Britain re-elect Prime Minister Margaret Thatcher for an historic third consecutive term.

Friday 12
Canadian athletes Ben Johnson and Angella Issajenko have won the 100-m events at an international track-and-field meet in Verona, Italy.
☆ 1921 — birth of James Houston, author-illustrator of *Frozen Fire*

JUNE

Saturday
13
Benji, canine star of Disney movies, is touring Canada to promote his (really her) latest film. She enjoys breakfast in an elegant Toronto restaurant. Menu: cottage cheese, sirloin steak (medium-well), Evian water and vanilla Haagen-Dazs ice cream.
☆ **1924** — birth of Harold Town, artist

Sunday
14
Muscleman David Gauder has pulled a 91-t Concorde aircraft to raise money for charity. Attached to the jet with a body harness, Gauder moved it 0.6 m. Ouch!
☆ **1924** — birth of Arthur Erickson, award-winning architect

Monday
15
In New York City, Canadian T.V. commercials win Clio Awards for advertising excellence. The subjects were Chiclets and Canadian tourism.
☆ **1789** — birth of Josiah Henson, founder of an Ontario community for fugitive slaves

Tuesday
16
Heatwave! Forest-fire crews are on alert as Ontario and the southeastern Prairies suffer from a record heatwave. Temperatures, normally 25°C, are as high as 35°C, and crops are endangered.
☆ **1874** — birth of Arthur Meighen, ninth prime minister of Canada

Wednesday
17
The same Leonardo da Vinci who painted the Mona Lisa and designed flying machines also designed gadgets to crush garlic, slice eggs, dry napkins and stretch lasagna. Montreal's Museum of Fine Arts is exhibiting his designs.

Thursday
18
Junior shareholders and their parents attended the annual meeting of Irwin Toy Ltd. to test the latest products. These included Yawnies (cuddly plush animals) and plenty of Zaks (snap-lock construction pieces).
☆ **1966** — birth of Kurt Browning, figure skating champion

Friday
19
The Metro (Toronto) Caravan, a nine-day multicultural fair, opens. Forty-three pavilions throughout the city celebrate people and countries around the world.
☆ **1902** — birth of Guy Lombardo, musician and conductor, world-famous for his New Year's Eve television celebrations

Saturday
20
Travellers are invited to be the first to see the sunrise at Cape Spear National Historic Park in Newfoundland, North America's easternmost point.
☆ **1857** — birth of Sir Adam Beck, who built and expanded hydroelectric service in Ontario

Sunday
21
Summer Solstice
A British meat-products factory has produced the world's longest sausage, measuring almost 16 km. It took 21 hours to prepare and was fried in pans 8 m in diameter. The sausage was eaten by 100 000 youngsters.

June

Monday 22
Tom Seaver, three-time winner of baseball's Cy Young Award for pitchers, announces his plans to retire from baseball because of a knee injury. This marks the end of his 19-year career in professional baseball.

Tuesday 23
Ling-Ling has given birth to a cub weighing 113 g at the U.S. National Zoo in Washington, D.C. The 18-year-old, 113-kg panda and her new cub are being closely monitored; Ling-Ling had also given birth to a stillborn cub.
☆ **1909** — birth of David Lewis, former leader of the New Democratic Party and one of Parliament's most powerful debaters

Wednesday 24
La Fête de la Saint-Jean-Baptiste
The Canadian Football League has announced the collapse of the Montreal Alouettes.
☆ **1855** — birth of Thomas Ahearn, believed to be the inventor of the electric stove

Thursday 25
A Vancouver company has perfected a tanning process that converts fish skins into leather for clothing, shoes, handbags and luggage.
☆ **1952** — birth of Tololwa Mollel, author of *The Orphan Boy*

Friday 26
Chinese scientists have discovered the fossil of a new dinosaur that lived more than 130 million years ago. They have named the dinosaur *Qagan Nur Dinosaur*, after the soda-factory site where it was found. When living, the dinosaur was 23 m long and nearly 7 m tall.
☆ **1854** — birth of Sir Robert Borden, eighth prime minister of Canada

Saturday 27
Ling-Ling's cub dies. Experts believe the cub would have been the first panda bred in captivity in the United States.

Sunday 28
At 21 years of age, Matthew Hilton has become the first Canadian-born world boxing champion in 44 years. He won the International Boxing Federation junior middleweight title in Montreal.

Monday 29
What a bookmark! Deborah Anderson unfolded a piece of paper tucked into a book she bought for four dollars at a Mississauga, Ontario, flea market — and got lucky. It was an authentic letter written by Albert Einstein in 1948. In the letter he pleaded with atomic scientists to avert nuclear war.

Tuesday 30
The one-dollar coin, called a loonie, is introduced across Canada.
☆ **1948** — birth of Murray McLauchlan, pop and country singer

JULY

Extra! Extra!

Boy Flies Plane Across the United States

Ten-year-old Christopher Marshall landed in the record books as the youngest pilot to fly across the U.S. Christopher flew a single-engine Piper Warrior from California to Florida in five days. He snacked on 48 candy bars and two boxes of cereal during the flight and sat on three pillows to see out of the cockpit window. When he grows up, Christopher wants to be … a pilot.

Whistle While You Work

Walt Disney first released the movie *Snow White* 50 years ago this month. It took 750 artists and technicians three years to come up with the right combination of characters, and even then there were problems. Walt Disney tested 150 actresses before he found the perfect voice for Snow White. And Dopey was supposed to have a voice, but Disney couldn't find one he liked, so Dopey doesn't say anything in the movie.

Trivia tidbit
There were 5.9 million homes with cable television in Canada in 1987.

You said it!
"You're on a wild goose chase." Long ago, a wild goose chase was a game of follow-the-leader played on horseback. The players rode in formation behind a leader, like flying geese. Today, a wild goose chase is a hopeless or foolish search.

What's *that*?!? Head-Smashed-In-Buffalo-Jump

A historic site where the Plains people once drove buffalo over low cliffs, Head-Smashed-In-Buffalo-Jump, in Alberta, is *not* named for the buffalo. Legend says that a Native boy wanted to know what he'd see if he stood at the bottom of the cliff as the buffaloes hurtled over. He was found later under a pile of buffaloes.

Wednesday
1
Canada Day
Buckingham Palace celebrates Canada Day for the first time. The Ontario Youth Concert Band entertains the Queen Mother and 1000 guests in the courtyard.
☆ **1952** — birth of Dan Aykroyd, actor

Thursday
2
In Whitehorse, Yukon Territory, a company will open North America's first arctic char farm. Char, an Inuit food staple, is a gourmet treat elsewhere in the world.
☆ **1821** — birth of Sir Charles Tupper, sixth prime minister of Canada

Friday
3
The Liberator is a new Canadian product that only *looks* like a wheelbarrow. It is actually an all-terrain wheelchair for physically challenged campers.
☆ **1870** — birth of Richard Bennett, 11th prime minister of Canada

JULY

Saturday 4
Screams from 50 000 fans fill the air as Madonna performs in Toronto. One million copies of her album *True Blue* have sold in Canada.
☆ **1887** — birth of Tom Longboat, long-distance runner

Sunday 5
Snow White, one of Disney's classic films, is all spiffed up and will be re-released soon to celebrate its 50th birthday.
☆ **1943** — birth of Robbie Robertson, singer and songwriter

Monday 6
Grab a pail and shovel! Some of the Great Lakes have lower water levels than last year, so there's more sand for sand-castles.
☆ **1948** — birth of Lydia Bailey, author of *Mother Nature Takes a Vacation*

Tuesday 7
Rock star Gino Vannelli visits Edmonton and Calgary as part of Disons Non Canada/Just Say No, a national anti-drug program.

Wednesday 8
Canada's first professional female umpire, Wilda Widmeyer, of Ontario, retires from amateur baseball after more than 50 seasons.

Thursday 9
Eye-popping colours, crazy patterns and cartoon-themed clothes are all the rage with kids nowadays. Mickey Mouse and Donald Duck are everywhere!

Friday 10
It's 41°C in Toronto, but Greg Lee is cool as … ice cream. He wears a parka for his job in a -23°C walk-in freezer full of ice cream.
☆ **1914** — birth of Joe Shuster, cartoonist and creator of "Superman"

Saturday 11
Whitehorse prospector Thomas Eckervogt pans for gold and finds a lump the size of a baked potato. The gold is valued at $75 000.
☆ **1950** — birth of Liona Boyd, classical guitarist

Sunday 12
Baby 5 Billion, Matej Gaspar, is born in Yugoslavia. By the time Matej is 12 1/2 years old, the world's population will reach 6 billion.
☆ **1920** — birth of Pierre Berton, author of *City of Gold*

Monday 13
This summer is hotter than usual. To beat the heat, people are drinking clear, bubbly, "New York style" seltzers.
☆ **1934** — birth of Peter Gzowski, radio host

Tuesday 14
Two Canadian women, Toni Sharpless and Kathleen Coburn, are revved up to enter the Suzuka, an eight-hour-long motorcycle race in Japan. They have tried to raise their body temperatures so that they can withstand Japan's 40°C heat.
☆ **1912** — birth of Northrop Frye, critic and professor

Wednesday 15
Andrew and Sarah, the Duke and Duchess of York, begin a 24-day trip in Canada.

Thursday 16
Forget the Velcro! Lace-up sneakers are back in style. Other foot favourites include variations on ballet and jazz shoes.

Friday 17
Tiny halogen light bulbs, one-tenth the size of a regular bulb, are generating a lot of interest — and more light than the old standbys.
☆ **1935** — birth of Donald Sutherland, actor

July

Saturday 18
A Superman exhibit at the Smithsonian Institution, in Washington, D.C., kicks off a year of super events celebrating Superman's 50th year.

Sunday 19
Alberta Blackfoot cartoonist Everett Soop wants to use animation to teach the Blackfoot language to children.
☆ 1950 — birth of Jocelyn Lovell, champion cyclist

Monday 20
The Bruce Peninsula, in Ontario, becomes Canada's newest national park. The park includes Canada's first marine park and two provincial parks.

Tuesday 21
Canadian Karen Dowell has won at the International Karate Association World Cup meet — she's been learning karate for only two years!
☆ 1926 — birth of Norman Jewison, film director

Wednesday 22
Northeastern New Brunswick will soon have more radio music. Licences have been approved for popular and soft-rock French-language stations.
☆ 1942 — birth of Kady MacDonald Denton, illustrator of *Til All the Stars Have Fallen*

Thursday 23
The Duke and Duchess of York officially open the World Heritage Site at Head-Smashed-In-Buffalo-Jump, Alberta, and receive a stuffed buffalo head.

Friday 24
Shells of dinosaur eggs found in Colorado are believed to be 145 million years old, the oldest ever discovered.
☆ 1899 — birth of Dan George, also known as Teswahno, actor

Saturday 25
Seth Scholes, of Kingston, Ontario, earns up to $30 a day by playing his saxophone on a street corner. The 11-year-old is trying to earn enough money to go to a David Bowie concert in Ottawa.
☆ 1930 — birth of Maureen Forrester, opera singer

Sunday 26
Rock stars get fit! Bryan Adams jogs; Rush musicians cycle; Tina Turner, Mick Jagger and Madonna run and exercise to build energy for their tours.

Monday 27
People in some parts of British Columbia and Ontario can now use their home computers to search their libraries' catalogue files and to reserve books.

Tuesday 28
Save that cash! In 1977, Levi's jeans were $17.95. Now they cost $42.00.
☆ 1958 — birth of Terry Fox, Marathon of Hope runner

Wednesday 29
Marathon swimmer Jocelyn Muir becomes the first person to swim the Tonawanda to Oswego section of the Erie Canal.

Thursday 30
The Canadian Baseball Hall of Fame is the new owner of five baseballs signed by Babe Ruth. People donated them after a ball hit by the Babe was stolen from the hall of fame in May.

Friday 31
Ripper! Fans of the film *Crocodile Dundee* are scooping up Australian gear. Drover coats and Akubra hats are everywhere.

AUGUST

Extra! Extra!

Frisbees: 30 Years of Flying

Other fads have come and gone, but the Frisbee is 30 years old this year. The simple plastic flying disc is available in dozens of different versions, ranging from the basic model to the more expensive types used by the experts in Frisbee competitions.

People disagree about the origin of the Frisbee, but many believe it goes back to the 1920s. Students at Yale University used to toss metal pie tins from the Frisbie Baking Company to each other and yell "Frisbie!" In the 1950s, Wham-O introduced the Frisbee ... and today, millions are sold around the world.

Top *T.V. Programs* 1987

- "The Cosby Show"
- "A Different World"
- "Cheers"
- "Growing Pains"
- "Night Court"
- "The Golden Girls"
- "Who's the Boss?"
- "60 Minutes"
- "Murder, She Wrote"
- "The Wonder Years"

Trivia tidbit

A blueberry pie measuring 1.83 m across and weighing more than 135 kg was cut into 1000 pieces at the 1987 Festival of Blueberries in Mistassini, Quebec.

What's *that*?!?   Scull

A scull is a small lightweight racing boat used by one or more rowers, or scullers. World professional sculling championships have been around since at least 1831.

You said it!

"Don't throw in the sponge."

Long ago, boxers were refreshed between rounds with a damp sponge. If the fighter didn't want to continue the match, his helper threw the sponge into the air. Ever since, the expression has been used to encourage someone not to surrender.

AUGUST

Saturday 1
In Toronto, more than half a million people watch the Caribana parade, which features 26 bands and 6000 dancing paraders. Caribana celebrates the spirit of the Caribbean.

Sunday 2
The Festival of Blueberries in Mistassini, Quebec, begins. For the next nine days, everything will be blue: lampposts, fences, clothing, even lipstick!

Monday 3
Civic Holiday
Loonies are so popular that people are hoarding them as collector's items — fewer are found in cash registers.
☆ **1951** — birth of Marcel Dionne, hockey player

Tuesday 4
During a ten-day canoe trip near Atikokan, Ontario, a troop of boy scouts rescues an injured bald eagle and cares for the endangered bird while they find help.
☆ **1877** — birth of Tom Thomson, painter and member of the Group of Seven

Wednesday 5
Wearing her trademark good-luck penguin badge, marathon swimmer Vicki Keith dives into Lake Ontario. She hopes to make a double crossing of the lake.
☆ **1961** — birth of Linda Hendry, illustrator of *The Amazing Potato Book*

Thursday 6
Hiroshima Day
The latest statistics show that Canadians born in the 1980s will live longer thanks to better health care. Girls could live to be 79 and boys, 72.

Friday 7
Lady of the Lake Vicki Keith completes her two-way crossing of Lake Ontario 56 hours after she began — it is the first non-stop two-way crossing. Vicki lost 18 kg during the journey.
☆ **1965** — birth of Elizabeth Manley, Olympic figure skater

Saturday 8
About 6000 fans crowd the streets of St Sauveur, Quebec, to see their idol, singer René Simard, marry Marie-Josée Taillefer.
☆ **1947** — birth of Ken Dryden, hockey player

Sunday 9
In Scarborough, Ontario, Cliff Thorburn wins the Canadian snooker championship for the fourth consecutive time.
☆ **1845** — birth of Brother André, Quebec religious counsellor

Monday 10
Holiday's over! The Duke and Duchess of York head back to Britain after two weeks of canoeing in the Arctic wilderness.

Tuesday 11
Join the club — 3 million Canadians already have. More and more fitness clubs are springing up across Canada. It's a fitness craze!

Wednesday 12
Ryan Smith, 4, and his dad have found a gigantic puffball on their farm near Guelph, Ontario. The fungus measures 1.93 m around — the world record is 1.94 m — and weighs 1.3 kg.
☆ **1935** — birth of Brian Doyle, author of *Easy Avenue*

AUGUST

Thursday 13
Calgary's Mark Tewksbury wins the gold medal in the 100-m backstroke at the Pan Pacific swim meet in Brisbane, Australia.

Friday 14
Canada wins again! Victor Davis, of Guelph, Ontario, wins the gold medal in the 100-m breaststroke at the Pan Pacific swim meet.
☆ **1931** — birth of Brenda Bellingham, author of *The Curse of the Silver Box*

Saturday 15
Back-to-school shopping begins. Fashion forecasts predict denim, big sweaters, practical knapsacks and cartoon designs on clothes.
☆ **1925** — birth of Oscar Peterson, jazz pianist

Sunday 16
The nine-day Upper Richelieu Hot Air Balloon Festival, in Quebec, closes. The balloon festival, Canada's largest, included 115 balloons from nine countries. One entry looked like a thatched-roof cottage.

Monday 17
Toronto's Silken Laumann has won gold in the women's single sculls at the Pan American Games in Indianapolis, Indiana. She finished an amazing 23 seconds ahead of the nearest rival.
☆ **1964** — birth of Colin James, singer-songwriter

Tuesday 18
In Paris, it's time to clean up after storms blew 150 000 t of sand from Africa's Sahara Desert into France.

Wednesday 19
The 109th Canadian National Exhibition opens in Toronto. The two-week fair features an exhibit from the People's Republic of China.

Thursday 20
British Columbia is in the middle of an election — to pick the official provincial bird. Favourites include the herring gull, crow, dodo and loon, but the winner will not be named until October. The province will be the sixth to adopt an official bird.
☆ **1957** — birth of Cindy Nicholas, marathon swimmer

Friday 21
Say "Mama" … Maria Olivera, of Buenos Aires, Argentina, has given birth to her 32nd child, a boy.

Saturday 22
Canadian and Russian teams are training together for a ski trip across the North Pole in 1988. The teams are sharing information and food specialties such as camel's milk and lamb's entrails. Yummy!
☆ **1943** — birth of Vlasta van Kampen, illustrator of *Orchestranimals*

AUGUST

Sunday 23
Look up. Look out! A large sphere filled with scientific instruments has fallen from the sky into a muddy field near Hairy Hill, Alberta. The sphere is part of a NASA experiment and will be trucked to Maryland for research.

Monday 24
People are already talking about a movie that won't be in the theatres for almost another year. *Who Framed Roger Rabbit* has both live action *and* animation. And for the first time, Donald Duck and Daffy Duck, characters from two different movie studios, will share the same screen.
☆ **1920** — birth of Alex Colville, painter

Tuesday 25
To beat the summer heat in Beijing, China, people slurp their way through millions of kilograms of watermelon. (It's all right to spit the seeds into the street.)
☆ **1869** — birth of C.W. Jefferys, painter and illustrator

Wednesday 26
A salvage team releases photos of the *Titanic,* which sank on April 14, 1912. Some of the ship's dishes are on the ocean floor, and officials believe that they took two hours to fall nearly 4000 m to the seabed — not one dish is cracked.
☆ **1957** — birth of Rick Hansen, wheelchair athlete

Thursday 27
Hockey superstar Wayne Gretzky is the new national spokesperson for the Council on Drug Abuse, a group that alerts parents and kids to the dangers of drugs.

Friday 28
Canadian-made T.V. programs are doing well: "The Raccoons" and "Degrassi Junior High" are being shown during peak viewing hours across North America.
☆ **1913** — birth of Robertson Davies, novelist

Saturday 29
Jocelyn Muir finishes her record-breaking 966-km swim around Lake Ontario. For 60 days she swam in water so cold that she had to wear three swimming caps and two sets of insulated boots.

Sunday 30
Double scullers Heather Hattin and Janice Mason win Canada's first-ever gold medal in women's rowing at the world championships in Copenhagen, Denmark.

Monday 31
The oldest existing Micmac Indian canoe has been returned to Canada after being away for 109 years! The 5.5-m canoe was sent to the Paris World's Fair in 1878, but is back in Canada for an exhibition of Native artifacts at Calgary's Glenbow Museum during the 1988 Winter Olympics.
☆ **1939** — birth of Dennis Lee, author of *Alligator Pie*

SEPTEMBER

Extra! Extra!

Ogopogo Still Making Waves

Canada's famous sea monster, Ogopogo, has been in the news since it first appeared in Lake Okanagan 127 years ago. Recently, a Japanese camera crew has been looking for him (or is it her?), and a B.C. inventor says he'll lure Ogie to the surface with heavy-metal music blasting from a submersible robot he has built. There's a $10 000 prize for anyone who captures Ogie alive.

Two Smart Cookies

When Lance Lehman and John Waldron were 11 years old, they founded Teddy's Chocolate Cookies. The two Guelph, Ontario, boys sold their cookies door-to-door. That was five years ago. Now the young men sell over 5000 cookies a week in seven large cities — and they still have time for school and sports!

Trivia tidbit

In Canada, 40 000 boats are manufactured each year for the 53 per cent of all Canadians who boat.

You said it!

"A little bird told me." People have believed since ancient times that birds are secret sources of information. Today, when people don't want to tell how they know something, they say that a little bird told them.

What's *that*?!?   Macaw

A macaw is a tropical American parrot with a long sword-shaped tail, powerful curved bill and brightly coloured feathers. The bird's name may come from the Portuguese word for the palm tree that grows the fruit the macaw eats.

Tuesday 1

In Nova Scotia, kids are visiting salons, not barbershops, for the latest back-to-school hairstyles. Girls are asking for french braids and puffy bangs. Boys want short spikes with plenty of gel.
☆ 1922 — birth of Yvonne DeCarlo, actress

Wednesday 2

Members of the California Angels and the Toronto Blue Jays square off in a bubble-gum-blowing contest. Jays pitcher Tom Henke wins with a face-covering bubble!

Thursday 3

Just peachy! Growers in B.C.'s Okanagan Valley expect to harvest 5443 t of the fuzzy fruit. Growers in Ontario's Niagara region plan to harvest 18 144 t.
☆ 1810 — birth of Paul Kane, artist

September

Friday 4
Simon the macaw knows 25 words — and he'll use every one of them as he sits on David Pederson's handlebars during a fundraising bicycle trip from Montreal to Toronto and back.

Saturday 5
Yogurt wows Canadians. Each year, Canadians eat an average of 3.2 kg of this ancient milk product.
☆ **1916** — birth of Frank Shuster, comedian and partner in Wayne and Shuster

Sunday 6
Martha, a 160-kg Russian tourist, enjoys a cookie on Halifax's Citadel Hill. As long as she gets cookies, Martha will skip rope and climb ladders. She's the oldest bear in the Moscow Circus, which is performing in Halifax.

Monday 7
Labour Day
A Swedish fan magazine is getting 1000 letters a week from fans of 18-year-old Yannick Bisson, the Canadian star of a miniseries being shown in Sweden.

Tuesday 8
Happy 35th birthday, CBC! There were just 146 000 television sets in Canada in 1952, when the Canadian Broadcasting Corporation began, and programs were on only between 7:00 P.M. and 10:30 P.M.

Wednesday 9
School has just reopened and trendy lunch-boxes are filled with bagels and peanut butter, rice cakes and drink boxes.

Thursday 10
Sandy McLachlin, 16, has become the first Canadian in 79 years to win the women's event at the world horseshoe championships in Wisconsin.

Friday 11
Oktoberfest '87 has opened in Winnipeg — in September! The annual German festival features lively music and dancing.
☆ **1940** — birth of Sue Ann Alderson, author of *Sure as Strawberries*

Saturday 12
Alberta wins big at the Canadian Country Music Awards in Vancouver. Cowboy crooner Ian Tyson wins three awards, and k.d. lang wins two.
☆ **1937** — birth of George Chuvalo, heavyweight boxing champion

Sunday 13
Hug a chair — it's the beginning of National Furniture Week.
☆ **1775** — birth of Laura Secord, heroine of the War of 1812

Monday 14
A fisherman in Ireland has found a balloon released from Scarborough, Ontario. Five-year-old Kortney Burgon let go of the balloon in May.
☆ **1940** — birth of Barbara Greenwood, author of *Spy in the Shadows*

Tuesday 15
The Canadian team wins the Canada Cup, beating the Soviet Union 6–5. Mario Lemieux scored the winning goal with only 86 seconds left in the game.

Wednesday 16
International Day of Peace
Chris White, of Whitby, Ontario, has won the Canadian youth dart championship in Winnipeg and will be off to England in December to compete in the world championships.

Thursday 17
Jacqui Brodie, of Mississauga, Ontario, is the second female to referee in the Metropolitan Toronto Hockey League.

SEPTEMBER

Friday 18
Home-delivered pizza is coming to Moscow, but food shortages mean that salt pork and black olives — with pits — might replace tomato sauce and cheese.
☆ **1895** — birth of John Diefenbaker, 13th prime minister of Canada

Saturday 19
The new television season is about to begin. New shows include "Full House," "Beauty and the Beast" and "Under the Umbrella Tree."
☆ **1940** — birth of Sylvia Tyson, singer-songwriter

Sunday 20
Pope John Paul II arrives in Fort Simpson, Northwest Territories, and 5000 Native Canadians greet him. The pope kept his promise to return — in 1984, his plane couldn't land at the historic trading post because of heavy fog.
☆ **1951** — birth of Guy Lafleur, hockey player

Monday 21
Canadian skating champion Brian Orser has started training for the Olympics next February by practising seven hours a day, five days a week.

Tuesday 22
The statue of King Edward VII, in Toronto, is being scrubbed, rinsed and waxed. The cleaning takes a week to do and costs $7000!

Wednesday 23
Autumn Equinox
The Sea-Doo, a water vehicle, bombed when it first came out in 1968, but its manufacturer is trying again. It hopes the speedy new version will be as successful as its Ski-Doo.

Thursday 24
Rosh Hashanah
Near Ottawa, Canada's tiniest baby is home. James Gill weighed 624 g when he was born, months early, in May. He set a record for surviving his low birth weight.

Friday 25
George, a dog celebrity, has been awarded the Toronto police commission's first Canine Award. The pooch fought off a pit bull terrier and an armed burglar.
☆ **1933** — birth of Ian Tyson, singer-songwriter

Saturday 26
A Montreal hockey-equipment manufacturer has designed a futuristic goalie helmet. The helmet has a communications link with coaches and radar that tracks pucks.

Sunday 27
The movie *The Princess Bride* is a huge hit around the country. "As you wish," an expression from the movie, is heard everywhere.
☆ **1948** — birth of Mark Thurman, author-illustrator of *One Two Many*

Monday 28
There aren't just books in those book bags — kids are taking action-figure toys to school with them, too. World Wrestling Federation heroes and G.U.T.S. and M.U.S.C.L.E. figures are the most popular.

Tuesday 29
A new stamp honouring the 50th anniversary of Air Canada features a jet flying over a globe.

Wednesday 30
Shoppers watch for a new product: "no-reek" garlic, for people with sensitive noses. Producers guarantee there'll be no fumes.

Extra! Extra!

Nessie Mystery Unsolved

While some scientists are in British Columbia looking for Ogopogo, others are in Scotland searching for Nessie, the Loch Ness Monster. In early October, sonar located "a very large lump" at the bottom of the lake, but after three days of searching, scientists still didn't have any answers. The only thing they discovered was that the "monster" that was photographed in 1975 was really a rotting tree stump 6 m below the loch's surface!

Thanksgiving

Many people believe that the Pilgrims' celebration in Massachusetts was the first Thanksgiving in North America. But historians say that the very first Thanksgiving Day in the New World was celebrated in Newfoundland by explorer Martin Frobisher in 1578 — long before the Pilgrims landed on Plymouth Rock.

Trivia tidbit

Eight-year-old Canadian T.V. star Sarah Polley has 24 pet toads and 236 tadpoles.

You said it!

"I'm mad as a hornet!" If hornets are disturbed, they will quickly sting whoever upset them. A person who is as mad as a hornet is very angry and ready to do something about it.

What's *that*?!?   Jack-o'-lantern

In the 1600s, a jack-o'-lantern was a night watchman who carried a lantern. ("Jack" was a nickname for any man.) Later, people started carving a face into a turnip or pumpkin and putting a lit candle inside, to light their way on Hallowe'en. These special Hallowe'en lanterns were soon called jack-o'-lanterns.

October

Thursday 1
High-school students in British Columbia will receive money for high marks. Good grades will earn students a stamp in a passport. At the end of high school, the passport can be redeemed for money to use for university.

Friday 2
Newfoundland author Kevin Major has mailed Bruce Springsteen a copy of his latest young adult novel, *Dear Bruce Springsteen*. Major hopes the Boss will reply.

Saturday 3
Yom Kippur
Jill is North America's first bilingual doll. She speaks French and English and has the voice of a real 12-year-old girl, thanks to a built-in minicomputer.
☆ 1927 — birth of Ashevak Kenojuak, Inuk artist

Sunday 4
Walk-a-dog-a-thons take place across Canada. The money will help buy guide dogs for people who are visually impaired.
☆ 1934 — birth of Rudy Wiebe, author

Monday 5
Four-year-old Mervyn Han has written to his school board in Winnipeg to ask if he can start school earlier. He's only in kindergarten, but he can already read Grade 2 books.
☆ 1965 — birth of Patrick Roy, hockey goaltender

Tuesday 6
Television star Mr Rogers and his puppets are visiting the Soviet Union. Daniel the tiger, one of Mr Rogers' puppets, is meeting Hryushka the piglet, a famous Russian puppet — their meeting will be caught on film!
☆ 1769 — birth of Sir Isaac Brock, hero of the War of 1812

Wednesday 7
SkyDome officials in Toronto decide that they will use a trained falcon to chase seagulls and pigeons out of the stadium when it's completed.

Thursday 8
Skinnamarink! "Sharon, Lois and Bram's Elephant Show" will now be seen in the U.S., where 35 million more people will be able to sing along.

Friday 9
Canadian comic actor Dan Aykroyd and his partners open a trendy restaurant, called X-Rays, in Toronto. (It's named after Aykroyd's friend, X-Ray MacRae.)

Saturday 10
Wheelchair athlete Rick Hansen marries Amanda Reid in Vancouver. Reid was Hansen's physiotherapist during his Man in Motion world tour.
☆ 1863 — birth of Louis Cyr, strongman

OCTOBER

Sunday
11
Bubble gum is the latest toothpaste flavour for kids. The toothpaste dispensers are decorated with stars and the words "super cool."
☆ **1929** — birth of Raymond Moriyama, architect

Monday
12
Thanksgiving
Crowds cheer for Queen Elizabeth II and Prince Phillip, who are travelling around Canada during a two-week stay.

Tuesday
13
It's Leftovers Day for many Canadians. Food columnists recommend using leftover turkey in tacos and stir-frys for something a little different.
☆ **1955** — birth of Jane Siberry, singer-songwriter

Wednesday
14
Baby authority Dr Benjamin Spock advises parents to start their children dusting and tidying the house when they are as young as two years old.
☆ **1916** — birth of Andrew Mynarski, World War II hero who earned a Victoria Cross for his bravery

Thursday
15
In Halifax, 15-year-old Jamie Lamond makes friends with a piglet at the Atlantic Winter Fair and has his picture snapped for the local paper.
☆ **1701** — birth of Marie-Marguerite d'Youville, founder of the Sisters of Charity of the Hôpital Général in Montreal

Friday
16
Seven-year-old Illya Woloshyn stars in *Jacob Two-Two Meets the Hooded Fang*. The play, which is based on the classic children's book, is playing in Toronto.

Saturday
17
Sarah, the Duchess of York, has inspired millions of North American women to be proud of their red hair. Red is hot, blond is not.
☆ **1948** — birth of Margot Kidder, actress

Sunday
18
Queen Elizabeth II watches a display of Great Plains Cree dancing and singing at Wanuskewin Park, near Saskatoon.
☆ **1919** — birth of Pierre Elliott Trudeau, 15th prime minister of Canada

Monday
19
The Royal Canadian Mint announces that the loonie is an absolute success. Eighty million coins are in circulation, and dollar bills will be gone by 1989.

Tuesday
20
Take a deep breath! Environment Canada gives Halifax top marks for its clean air — it ranks first out of 35 Canadian cities.
☆ **1873** — birth of Nellie McClung, reformer and women's rights advocate

OCTOBER

Wednesday 21
About 2000 Native students of all ages protest on Parliament Hill, demanding more money for education.

Thursday 22
Curtis Hibbert, of Mississauga, Ontario, becomes the first Canadian to qualify for a world championship apparatus final at the world gymnastic championships in Rotterdam. Curtis received a near-perfect 9.9 score from the judges.
☆ **1844** — birth of Louis Riel, Metis leader and founder of Manitoba

Friday 23
Adventurer Gary Sowerby, of Moncton, New Brunswick, has set a new record for long-distance driving. He drove from the tip of South America to the Arctic Circle in just 23 days.
☆ **1963** — birth of Gordon Korman, author of *Losing Joe's Place*

Saturday 24
Tonight's the night to turn clocks back an hour — unless you live in Saskatchewan, the only province that doesn't recognize daylight saving time.

Sunday 25
A new stamp commemorates the Ninth Commonwealth Heads of Government Meeting, which was held recently in Vancouver.

Monday 26
Members of Toronto's Greek community continue to celebrate the first annual Greek Culture Month.

Tuesday 27
What a jack-o'-lantern! In Whitby, Ontario, Darcy Parker and his sister Yvette have grown a 91-kg pumpkin. They were too late to enter the veggie in a contest, so they sold it to a store for $35.
☆ **1946** — birth of Ivan Reitman, film director

Wednesday 28
Three Canadian T.V. shows take all the nominations in the children's category at the Emmy Awards: "Degrassi Junior High," "Fraggle Rock" and "The Man Who Planted Trees."

Thursday 29
Canadian star Sarah Polley, 8, is playing her favourite book character, Ramona Quimby, in a ten-part T.V. series.
☆ **1926** — birth of Jon Vickers, opera singer

Friday 30
Alex Baumann, who won two gold medals for swimming at the 1984 Summer Olympics, announces his retirement. He is 23 years old.
☆ **1930** — birth of Timothy Findley, author

Saturday 31
Hallowe'en
Costumed kids take to the streets and fill the air with their calls, "Shell out!"
☆ **1950** — birth of John Candy, actor

Extra! Extra!

Cooking by Volcano

Residents on the Azores island of São Miguel are tapping into volcanic energy—and eating well, too. The Earth's crust is very thin on this volcanic island, so heat and steam from the Earth's core are close to the surface. People take advantage of this by wrapping food in cloth and burying it in the ground. Hours later, the slowly cooked food is removed. People claim that the food is healthier because it has absorbed rich minerals from the nearby thermal springs. The island is one big pressure cooker.

Top Movies 1987

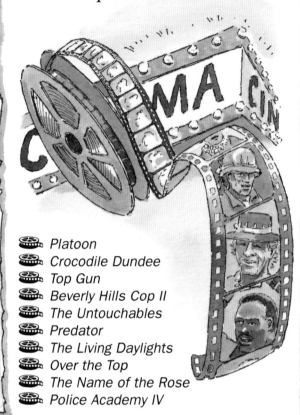

- *Platoon*
- *Crocodile Dundee*
- *Top Gun*
- *Beverly Hills Cop II*
- *The Untouchables*
- *Predator*
- *The Living Daylights*
- *Over the Top*
- *The Name of the Rose*
- *Police Academy IV*

Trivia tidbit

During its 88-day journey to Calgary, the Olympic torch will be carried by 6520 people. The torch weighs 1.7 kg and is 60 cm long.

What's *that*?!?   Lemon grass

Used in Vietnamese cooking, lemon grass is a grass-like plant with a bulb at one end. The plant has a hint of lemon fragrance.

You said it!

"What a white elephant!"
An old legend said that only the King of Siam could own white elephants, which were rare and very expensive to keep. So when the king was angry at someone, he gave a white elephant to that person, who was soon ruined. Today, a white elephant is something a person no longer wants.

NOVEMBER

Sunday 1
The new Christmas stamps are ready. They feature a holly wreath, mistletoe, a poinsettia and gifts under a fir tree. Ho! ho! ho!
☆ **1949** — birth of David Foster, singer-songwriter

Monday 2
Bryan Adams, k.d. lang, Luba and Rita MacNeil are some of the Juno Award winners. Bill Usher's album for kids, *Drums,* scores, too.
☆ **1961** — birth of k.d. lang, singer-songwriter

Tuesday 3
Work has started in France on the English Channel tunnel that will link France and Britain with an undersea railway. The first trains are planned to enter the tunnel in 1993.
☆ **1922** — birth of Bernice Thurman Hunter, author of *That Scatterbrain Booky*

Wednesday 4
People are learning that there's more than one kind of squash. This fall, recipes are featuring Hubbard, acorn, butternut, buttercup, spaghetti, banana, Sweet Mama and Kabocha squashes.

Thursday 5
Guitarist Jeff Healey and his band invite the public to "act" like an audience for three hours while they tape a video of "My Little Girl" in a Toronto club.
☆ **1959** — birth of Bryan Adams, singer-songwriter

Friday 6
Jodi Weiss, 4, of Scarborough, Ontario, is kicked off the Three Little Pigs boys hockey team because she's a girl — a rule's a rule.
☆ **1867** — birth of Joseph Boyle, "Klondike Joe," adventurer

Saturday 7
Officials reverse yesterday's decision. Jodi Weiss is allowed to play on the Three Little Pigs boys hockey team. *She* helps them to a 4 – 4 tie.
☆ **1943** — birth of Joni Mitchell, singer-songwriter

Sunday 8
Can't get enough of comic books or cartoons? The Cartoon Museum, in Orlando, Florida, has 70 000 comic books and original cartoon art.

Monday 9
Canadian actress Megan Follows has been nominated for an American pay T.V. award for her performance in *Anne of Avonlea.*
☆ **1717** — birth of Louis-Joseph Gaultier de La Vérendrye, explorer

Tuesday 10
What a fish story! Bobby Smith, 12, and Matthew Gallaher, 11, pose proudly with the 17-kg and 13-kg salmon they caught near Toronto with their bare hands.
☆ **1845** — birth of Sir John Thompson, fourth prime minister of Canada

NOVEMBER

Wednesday
11
Remembrance Day
In memory of the men and women who died in World Wars I and II, two minutes of silence are observed across the country at the 11th hour of the 11th day of the 11th month.

Thursday
12
The trendy toys for Christmas 1987 include Cricket, a doll that sings and tells jokes; Pound Puppies; the Heart Family; Get in Shape Girl exercise equipment and Thundercats action figures.
☆ **1606** — birth of Jeanne Mance, founder of the Hôtel-Dieu hospital in Montreal

Friday
13
A battery that's as thin and flexible as a piece of paper has been invented in Japan. So far, it can only be used in appliances — battery-guzzling toys will have to wait!

Saturday
14
The Calgary Olympic Organizing Committee has arrived in Athens, Greece. The members of the committee will bring the Olympic flame from Olympus, Greece, to Canada.
☆ **1891** — birth of Sir Frederick Banting, co-discoverer of insulin

Sunday
15
Torontonians line the streets for 6.5 km and watch 1200 costumed people, 21 floats and 20 bands in the 82nd Annual Santa Claus Parade.
☆ **1969** — birth of Helen Kelesi, tennis player

Monday
16
The Olympic flame arrives in Gander, Newfoundland, in *two* miner's lamps — just in case something happens to the first lamp.
☆ **1957** — birth of Barbara Reid, author-illustrator of *Two By Two*

Tuesday
17
St John's welcomes the Olympic flame. The torch is lit and its 18 000-km journey to Calgary begins. Danielle O'Keefe, 10, is the youngest of the 63 torchbearers in Newfoundland.
☆ **1938** — birth of Gordon Lightfoot, singer-songwriter

Wednesday
18
Outfielder George Bell, of the Toronto Blue Jays, has been named the American League's most valuable player.
☆ **1939** — birth of Margaret Atwood, author

Thursday
19
Patients at the Hospital for Sick Children, in Toronto, cheer up as SICO drops by for a visit. The robot is a movie star — it appeared with Sylvester Stallone in *Rocky IV*.
☆ **1937** — birth of Marilyn Bell, marathon swimmer

NOVEMBER

Friday
20

A football flies through the air on the new stamp issued to mark the 75th Grey Cup game.
☆ **1841** — birth of Sir Wilfrid Laurier, seventh prime minister of Canada

Saturday
21

Siluck Saysanasy, 13, plays Yick Yu on "Degrassi Junior High," but he plans to be a doctor, not an actor, when he's older. Saysanasy came to Canada from Laos, in southeast Asia, when he was five years old.
☆ **1902** — birth of Foster Hewitt, broadcaster

Sunday
22

Christmas-season movies are being released. Watch for *Teen Wolf Too*, Walt Disney's *Cinderella* and *Like Father, Like Son*, starring T.V. favourite Kirk Cameron.
☆ **1950** — birth of Linda Granfield, the author of this book

Monday
23

Nosey the lioness is recuperating from dental surgery. The operation was performed at the Metropolitan Toronto Zoo by two dentists who usually work only on humans. They said the worst part of the job was Nosey's bad breath.

Tuesday
24

Vietnamese food is becoming very popular. Grocery stores and restaurants stock up on fish sauce, lemon grass, rice paper and shrimp chips.

Wednesday
25

The movie *Three Men and a Baby*, filmed in Ontario earlier this year, opens in theatres.

Thursday
26

Hurry! Hurry! Officials say there are only 650 000 tickets left for events at the 1988 Winter Olympics — 1.2 million tickets have already been sold.
☆ **1938** — birth of Rich Little, impressionist

Friday
27

Barbie is still queen of the dolls. Her competition — Jem and her singing partners, the Holograms — will not be produced any more because Barbie has her *own* rock band.

Saturday
28

The Niagara Falls International Winter Festival of Lights opens. Visitors can see over 100 trees decorated with lights and 17 animated displays by the famous falls.
☆ **1949** — birth of Paul Shaffer, musician

Sunday
29

It's Grey Cup Day! In Vancouver, the Edmonton Eskimos beat the Toronto Argonauts 38–36.
☆ **1941** — birth of Denny Doherty, singer-songwriter with the Mamas and the Papas

Monday
30

Forget hockey and volleyball. High-school students are more interested in sports like archery, cricket, water polo, curling and table tennis.
☆ **1874** — birth of Lucy Maud Montgomery, author of *Anne of Green Gables*

DECEMBER

Extra! Extra!

Bald Eagle Crosses the Atlantic

A North American bald eagle landed in Ireland after flying about 6000 km across the Atlantic Ocean. Rangers found the eagle 20 km inland — the first bald eagle to be captured in Europe. The eagle was nursed for a few days before it was taken back to the United States.

Best-selling Albums in Canada 1987

♪ *Slippery When Wet,* Bon Jovi
♪ *The Joshua Tree,* U2
♪ *Whitney,* Whitney Houston
♪ *Bad,* Michael Jackson
♪ *True Blue,* Madonna

Trivia tidbit

The 3390 athletes, trainers and officials participating in the 1988 Calgary Winter Olympics are expected to consume about 250 beef cattle, 1000 kg of salmon and 45 trailer-loads of milk during the two weeks.

You said it!

"Bah, humbug!"
Scrooge, in Charles Dickens's *A Christmas Carol,* made this saying famous, but the origin of "humbug" is unclear. The expression means "Nonsense!"

What's *that*?!? Latkes

Latkes, or potato pancakes, are a traditional Jewish food served during Chanukah. They are made of potato, onion, flour and eggs. It's been said that *latkes* take longer to make than to eat.

Tuesday 1 Torchbearers carry the Olympic flame from New Brunswick into Quebec. Only 74 days remain in the countdown to the Calgary Winter Olympics.

Wednesday 2 The Italian Olympic team has received permission to bring its own food to Calgary: 800 kg of spaghetti, 10 kg of ham and 600 bottles of wine and olive oil.

Thursday 3 The Metropolitan Toronto Zoo welcomes three new alligators — Smiles, Chuckles and Elvis!
☆ **1917** — birth of Miriam Waddington, poet

Friday 4 Justine Blainey, 14, who was barred from playing on a boys hockey team, has won her case after a 2½-year-long legal battle. Any girl can try out for any amateur boys sports team.

December

Saturday 5
Scientists near Hamilton, Ontario, are studying the ruins of a house that dates from 1500 B.C. It is as old as Stonehenge, the ring of standing stones in England.

Sunday 6
Ian Wallace reveals the inspiration for *Morgan the Magnificent* — Morgan Haupt, 6, of North Vancouver. She is the daring high-wire walker in his new book.
☆ **1803** — birth of Susanna Moodie, author of *Roughing It in the Bush*

Monday 7
Professor Erno Rubik, inventor of Rubik's Cube, demonstrates his latest mindbender, Unlink the Rings. It looks easy, but …
☆ **1916** — birth of Jean Carignan, "Ti-Jean," fiddler

Tuesday 8
Kellie Watson, winner of the SkyDome name contest, selects her prize. Two front-row seats behind home plate are hers for every SkyDome event for life.

Wednesday 9
Eight monks at a monastery in Hockley Heights, Ontario, have baked more than 2268 kg of fruitcake to sell. That's a lot of sweetmeats!

Thursday 10
"Degrassi Junior High" fans celebrate — the show wins Best Children's Series at the Gemini Awards.

Friday 11
Holiday record sales boom. The biggest sellers are Michael Jackson's *Bad* and *The California Raisins Sing the Hit Singles*.
☆ **1964** — birth of Carolyn Waldo, Olympic synchronized swimmer

Saturday 12
Slimy, but very useful. Doctors are using leeches to help injured fingers heal. The leeches suck the blood out of the injured area and help the body make new blood vessels in the finger.

Sunday 13
Hockey superstar Wayne Gretzky admits that his relationship with American actress Janet Jones is "serious." Jones admits that she had never seen a hockey game before she met Gretzky.
☆ **1871** — birth of Emily Carr, artist

Monday 14
Canada Post officials announce that letters to Santa must be received at the North Pole by December 20 if children want an answer.

Tuesday 15
Cowboys Don't Cry, the film based on Albertan Marilyn Halvorson's young-adult novel, will have its world premiere at the 1988 Winter Olympics in Calgary.

Wednesday 16
Chanukah begins
Ottawa student Kristi Lambert carries the Olympic torch into the House of Commons before Olympic ceremonies begin at Parliament Hill.

Thursday 17
Gift suggestions for dogs and cats: custom sheepskin-lined black leather coats, all-natural doggie biscuits, sailor and tuxedo collars with bows.
☆ **1874** — birth of William Lyon Mackenzie King, tenth prime minister of Canada

Friday 18
Ernie Coombs, better known as Mr Dressup, celebrates 20 years on Canada's highest-rated children's show.
☆ **1961** — birth of Brian Orser, Olympic figure skater

December

Saturday 19
Hockey star Bobby Orr hosts his seventh annual skate-a-thon at Maple Leaf Gardens in Toronto. Darryl Sittler, Eddie Shack and Ron Ellis also skate in this charity event.

Sunday 20
Mohawk chief Earl Hill welcomes the Olympic torch to the Tyendinaga Indian Reserve, west of Kingston, Ontario.

Monday 21
Montreal native Carolyn Waldo is named Canadian Press female athlete of the year. The synchronized swimmer has been undefeated since winning the silver medal at the 1984 Summer Olympics.

Tuesday 22
Winter Solstice
This is the shortest day of the year — there are only 8 hours and 55 minutes of daylight.

Wednesday 23
Thousands line the streets to see the Olympic torch carried through Toronto.
☆ 1908 — birth of Yousuf Karsh, photographer

Thursday 24
The Olympic bobsleigh team from the U.S. Virgin Islands trained in the sand at home, but now they're enjoying Calgary's winter training conditions.
☆ 1900 — birth of Joey Smallwood, the premier of Newfoundland who led the province to Confederation

Friday 25
Christmas
Jingle Bell? From today until New Year's Day, over 600 Bell Canada operators will be on duty to handle long-distance calls to and from countries around the world.
☆ 1850 — birth of Isabella Valancy Crawford, author

Saturday 26
Boxing Day
Elementary! It's been 100 years since the first Sherlock Holmes story was published. A special medal has been designed to honour Holmes.

Sunday 27
Over 1000 Canadian teens head to Australia for the 16th World Scout Jamboree. On New Year's Eve, 14 000 scouts will open the jamboree.
☆ 1823 — birth of Sir Mackenzie Bowell, fifth prime minister of Canada

Monday 28
Actor Michael J. Fox visits patients at Vancouver Children's Hospital while in town seeing his family for the holidays.
☆ 1928 — birth of Janet Lunn, author of *Amos's Sweater*

Tuesday 29
Soviet cosmonaut Yuri Romanenko and his two crewmates end a record 326-day flight in space.

Wednesday 30
In Montreal, Dorchester Street has been renamed René Lévesque Boulevard in honour of Lévesque, a Québécois politician who passed away this year.
☆ 1869 — birth of Stephen Leacock, humorist

Thursday 31
The new year has been postponed — by one second. That second is needed to make up for a slowing of Earth's rotation that has put the planet behind time.
☆ 1947 — birth of Burton Cummings, singer-songwriter